For Tina – *AM*

To my son, Boris – *MCS*

First published in Great Britain in 1993
by Orion Children's Books
This edition first published in Great Britain 2005
By Orion Children's Books
a division of the Orion Publishing Group Ltd
Orion House
5 Upper St Martin's Lane
London WC2H 9EA

A catalogue record for this book is available from the British Library
Printed and bound in Italy
ISBN 1 84255 182 5

www.orionbooks.co.uk

FELIX AND THE BLUE DRAGON

By Angela McAllister

Illustrated by Mary Claire Smith

Orion
Children's Books

"But it can't be as wonderful as my treasure," said Felix. "I have a golden horn that can call all the creatures of the forest and the birds of the sky."

"Well, so have I," said the dragon. He fetched a golden horn from deep inside his cave.

When the dragon blew the horn a great galloping was heard, and all the creatures of the forest gathered round and the trees were filled with singing birds.

Felix the Prince rode on a red stag and the Blue Dragon danced with a unicorn.

"I have even more wonderful things," said the dragon. "I have a flag of rainbow silk that will stir up the four winds."

"So have I," said Felix. He ran home to his treasure chamber and returned with a shimmering silk flag.

When Felix the Prince waved the flag four breezes
swept across the forest floor.

With one gust they blew him into the air, over the treetops, towards the mountains. The dragon opened his wings and flew after Felix.

Together they soared above icy lakes and frozen waterfalls.

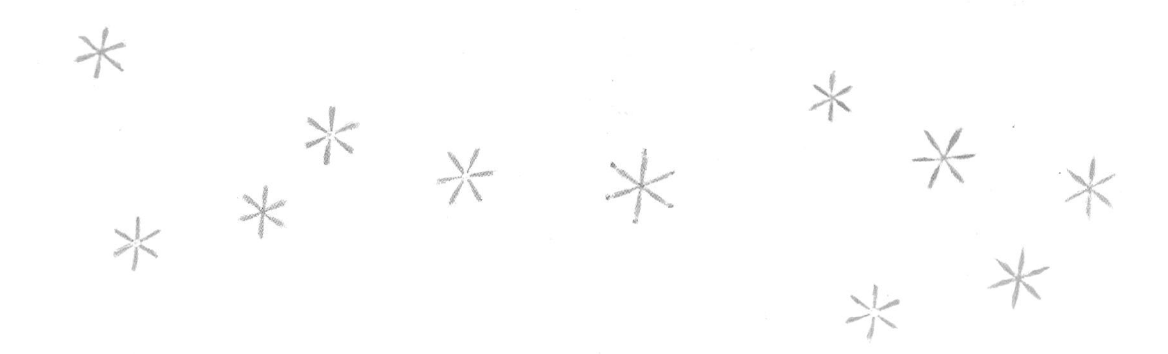

Then snowflakes began to fall.

The dragon let Felix ride on his warm back.

Back in the forest Felix stamped the snow from his shoes. "I have even more treasures," he declared. "I have a casket of powder that will fill the sky with fireworks."

"So have I," said the dragon, and he disappeared into his cave.

Soon he returned with a silver casket and flew in low circles above Felix, sprinkling powder on the grass.

Suddenly the sky grew dark and fireworks sprouted from the earth, shot high through the trees and exploded into stars. The Blue Dragon breathed spinning fireballs into the sky and Felix the Prince conducted the fireworks like a grand orchestra.

Slowly the fireworks died and the sky was blue again.

"Now, which one of us has the most wonderful treasure?" asked the dragon as Felix shook the sparkles from his hair.

"Let's both bring one more treasure," said Felix, "and then we shall see."

So the dragon set off down his long tunnel and Felix hurried back to the castle.

The treasure chamber was at the end of a long underground passage.

Felix counted one hundred steps to its door.

Meanwhile, the dragon went deeper and deeper into his cave until he reached a huge, heavy rock.

He rolled it aside just as Felix unbolted his chamber door and there they were …

… Felix and the dragon, face to face.

"This is *my* treasure!" cried Felix the Prince.

"But this is *my* treasure!" cried the Blue Dragon.

The underground chamber and the dragon's cave were the very same place.

They'd been sharing the same treasure all along.

"So we both have the most wonderful treasure in the land!" said the dragon.

Felix laughed. "We both have one thousand precious things."

From that day Felix, Prince of the Castle,
Prince of the Mountains, and Prince of the Forest,
shared the treasure with the Blue Dragon.
He never had to play with his shadow again.